WHERE IN TIME IS CARMEN SANDIEGO?/Part II®

Text by John Peel

Cover Illustration by Paul Vaccarello

Interior Illustrations by John Nez

Western Publishing Company, Inc.
Racine, Wisconsin 53404

Your Briefing

Congratulations — you've been hired as a rookie detective for the Acme Detective Agency. Your goal is to outsmart Carmen Sandiego and her gang by solving the cases in this book.

There are four cases to solve. Start by removing the cards from the middle of this book. Divide the cards into four groups. You should have the following:

4 Stolen Object Cards
4 Bookmark/Scorecards
8 Suspect Cards
8 Time Cards

Each case involves a stolen object. Decide which case you are going to solve by picking a **stolen object card**. Put the other stolen object cards away until you are ready to solve those cases.

Use a different **scorecard** for each case. As you read through each case, you will be given clues about the suspects. Write these clues down on your scorecard. Compare these clues to your **suspect cards.** Only one suspect will fit all the clues. Once you have picked a suspect, set aside the other cards until the next game.

Each time you are told to go to a different number

in the case, mark your **scorecard.** These are your travel points.

When you go to a new number, you may use the **scorecard as a bookmark** to hold your place while you're investigating — sometimes you will have to retrace your steps.

Use the **time cards** for information about the various places that you'll have to visit while tracking down a suspect.

HOW TO SCORE THE GAME:

To win, you must solve the case by finding the right suspect in the right place. You cannot win if you capture the wrong suspect. Once you've found the crook and the stolen object, add up your **total travel points.** Check this score on the last page to see if you've earned a promotion. You earn a promotion by capturing the crook and stolen object in as few moves as possible. The lower your total number of travel points, the more chances you have of earning a promotion.

Ready? Okay — put on your raincoat and hat and get ready to set off on a dangerous mission into the past for the Acme Detective Agency.

You're on your way to work at the Acme Detective Agency when you glance at your watch. It's stopped again. You always seem to have trouble with it. You remind yourself to buy a new one if your next bonus comes through. Meanwhile, you head for a jeweler's shop to get this old one repaired.

"This watch sure has taken a beating," the repairman says when he examines the watch.

"That's for sure," you agree. "Last night, when a crook attacked me, I took a blow on my arm. But fortunately I was able to arrest him."

"Well, no wonder the poor watch is not working," the repairman says. "It probably wants the reward money."

Suddenly the phone rings, and he answers it. Then the repairman looks up at you. "You don't happen to work for the Acme Detective Agency, do you?" he asks.

"Yeah."

He holds out the phone. "It's for you."

Puzzled, you take the receiver. It's your secretary. "How did you find me?" you ask.

"You're the detective, remember," she tells you. "You figure it out."

"So what's up?" you ask, ignoring her bad mood.

"Carmen and her gang have struck again."

You frown. "Aren't they doing time in San Quentin?"

"They were, but they broke out last night. This morning we got word that four of the greatest treasures of all time have been stolen."

"They didn't waste any time," you reply. "I guess it's time for me to check out the Chronoskimmer and go after them." This makes you really happy because you always enjoy using the time machine. "I'll be right over," you tell your secretary and hang up.

As you run for the door, the repairman yells: "What about your watch?"

"I don't have time for it right now!" you call back. "I'll pick it up tonight. Gotta fly."

Once in the office, you see that your secretary has put the latest files on Carmen's gang on your desk. You check out the escaped gang members and then get ready to track down the first stolen object.

If you want to look for:

The Viking longboat — go to #34

The Ming vase — go to #50

The Rubáiyát — go to #88

The Aztec temple — go to #130

The Chase

#1. Murasaki Shikibu is a very cheerful lady of the Japanese court. Her hair is carefully done up, and she wears an elegant kimono. As you ask her about the thief you're tracking, she serves you a cup of steaming tea.

"I saw the woman you seek," she replies. "She told me that she plans to visit a land that lies to the west of Japan."

You thank her for the tea and help, then head back to your Chronoskimmer, located at #135, to check out this clue.

#2. You've arrived in Greece in the 5th century B.C. It's the height of Greek civilization, but you're down in the dumps. Go to #72 to find out why you are in the wrong place.

#3. You've tracked Alexander Graham Edison to a Chinese government office building. Hmm, there's a job opening for director of dog catching. Seems like a good job, but you're not interested. Since you didn't make your catch, move along to #111 to find out what to do next.

#4. Pericles turns out to be a large, powerful man who looks every inch the ruler and soldier he is. Unfortunately, he's also rather arrogant and rude, so he's not well liked. When you meet him, you ask about the thief you're trailing.

Pericles glares at you. "I'm conducting a war with Sparta!" he yells. "I haven't time to worry about silly little problems! Get out of here before I have your head chopped off!"

You beat a hasty retreat in case he means it. Not much luck with this lead, so you decide to head back to #79 and look for another clue.

#5. The Chronoskimmer time machine lands you in West Africa in the 19th century. There's a lot going on here, with rulers trying to conquer huge empires. Everyone's much too busy to talk to you, so you'd better get along to #72 and find out why you seem to be in the wrong place.

#6. The Chronoskimmer comes to a halt and you find yourself in the Islamic world, sometime between the 8th and the 12th centuries. It stretches from China to Spain and from Russia to Africa. Though there are many rulers, they are all Muslims by faith. It's a period in which many scholars are supported by the rulers, and artists and carpet weavers create beautiful works. Though there are many wars, there is also a great deal of trading and learning.

The Chronoskimmer's computer beeps to let you know it has discovered some leads for you to look into.

If you want to talk to:
Saladin — go to #60
Nureddin — go to #119
Shirquh — go to #148

If you think the crook went to:
1st century B.C. Rome — go to #77
11th century England — go to #35
5th century B.C. Greece — go to #2

#7. You find the philosopher Plato teaching a group of students in his house. He's dressed in a simple robe and is almost bald. You can't make sense of what he's talking about — it's something to do with shadows cast by flames on a cave wall. When he sees you, he tells the class to take a break while he talks to you. They all look very relieved! You ask him about the crook you're trailing. You only hope you can understand his answer!

"Ah, the brown-eyed one," he says. "She was indeed here. She said something about going on to Asia next." He smiles. "Tell me, are you interested in studying logic?"

"If I am, I'll talk to Mr. Spock," you reply as Plato raises an eyebrow. You hurry back to your time machine at #19 to check out the clue he's given you.

#8. You've reached Rome in the 1st century B.C. It's a very busy place, and the citizens are preparing a victory parade for a returning general. Everyone's much too busy to talk to you, so you decide to move on to #72 to find out why you seem to be in the wrong place.

#9. You've tracked Lotta Style to a carpet maker's shop. The workers here are weaving a very elaborate carpet, covered with colors and patterns. But there's no sign of Lotta, so you've gotta go to #111.

#10. Horace is working on a new poem when you find him. He's considered one of the greatest Roman poets. He's also a favorite of the Emperor Augustus. He breaks off his writing to talk to you.

"Yes, I saw the scoundrel you're after," he says. "He said something about going west of here on his next trip." Then he sighs. "You aren't any good at poetry, are you?" he asks. "I'm stuck for a rhyme."

"I'm only good at limericks," you reply. "How's this: ☞

'There was a young lady named Carmen
Who would rob anyone but not harm 'em.
I'm devoted to crime
And would steal all the time,
But I don't think that violence is charmin'.'"

Horace sadly shakes his head. "Thanks, but don't call me, I'll call you."

You tip your hat and head back to the time machine at #168 to check out his clue.

#11. The Chronoskimmer lands in Kurdistan in the year 945. There are plenty of Kurds around, but you've lost your way. You better move on to #72 to find out why you arc in the wrong place.

#12. The Chronoskimmer brings you in to a gentle landing. You've reached England in the 11th century. It's a time of great trouble, with many warring armies fighting over the land. The Vikings are raiding the shores, and the Saxons are fighting among themselves. William of Normandy is waiting to invade the whole country, and there is fighting going on in Wales and Scotland. You've really landed in the middle of a mess!

Despite all that's going on, it's quite peaceful for the

moment. You jump when the time machine's computer beeps to let you know it's printed out your leads.

If you want to interview:
Edward the Confessor — *go to #92*
Earl Godwin — *go to #16*
Queen Edith — *go to #100*

If you think that the crook went to:
16th century Mexico — *go to #170*
14th century China — *go to #32*
5th century B.C. Greece — *go to #79*

#13. You arrive at the home of General Al-Haj 'Umar. It's 1804, and the general is planning a jihad (holy war) from his home country of Senegal. He hopes to unite all of Africa. His plans are top-secret, so his home is guarded by soldiers. They won't allow you to see him. "The general is busy," they growl. Finally you give up and decide to return to your home base at #29 and follow another lead!

#14. You arrive in England during the 11th century. You've come to King William's biggest castle, called the White Tower. This is the home of what will one day become the world-famous Tower of London. The grim Norman soldiers check to see that you're not armed, then escort you in to see the king. You explain to William that you're looking for the crook who stole a priceless Ming vase, and ask if he can help.

"I'm trying to rule this dreadful country," he explains. "I'm having terrible problems of my own. The English don't like me, and they're constantly fighting. I don't have time to worry about a silly stolen vase."

You thank him so he doesn't throw you in a dungeon. The Chronoskimmer's at #110, so you head back to follow a different lead.

#15. You've landed in Japan in the 12th century. After a long period of wars, the country is finally settling down. Unfortunately, your clues are still unsettled, so you'd better move on to #72 and discover why you are in the wrong place.

#16. It's England during the 11th century, and you find the Earl of the Saxons, Earl Godwin, in his fortress. He's busy plotting to make sure that when King Edward (also known as Edward the Confessor) dies, one of his children will rule all of England. The earl has married his daughter, Edith, to the king, and the earl's second oldest son, Harold, is favored to become the next ruler. But Earl Godwin has heard a rumor that Edward the Confessor promised the throne to a Frenchman named William of Normandy. Wow! This is better than a daytime soap opera.

You ask the earl about the crook you're after.

"I saw the man," he replies. "He has brown hair. And he said he'd planned on traveling east on his next trip."

You thank him and head back to your time machine at #12 to check out these clues.

#17. You've landed in the Islamic city of Baghdad, sometime between the 8th and 12th centuries. Baghdad is a rich city, bustling with activity. There are people here from all over the world — warriors and poets, priests and merchants. The town is packed. There are also many myths and legends about the city. But you see no sign of magic carpets or bottles with genies in them!

The computer beeps to tell you it's discovered three people in town who might be able to help you.

If you want to meet with:

Harūn ar-Rashid — *go to #122*

Scheherazade — *go to #59*

Yahya ibn Khālid — *go to #143.*

#18. You find Julius Caesar in the Roman Senate. He has just finished a speech to the ruling body of Rome and is getting a lot of applause. As soon as things quiet down, you make your way over to him. Although Caesar is liked by a lot of people, he is disliked by just as many. Some think he's making Rome stronger, and others think he's ruining the country. It's just like politics back home, you realize.

You catch Caesar's attention and ask about the crook you're looking for.

"He was here," Caesar tells you. "I think he was a little bit crazy. He said something about traveling through time almost a thousand years into the future. Isn't that just too silly for words?"

You don't let him know that you can travel through time as well. Better not have him think your brains are scrambled. He invites you to stay for lunch — Caesar's having a salad — but you tell him you have to rush. You head back to your Chronoskimmer (#77) to check out this clue.

#19. The Chronoskimmer time machine lands, and you look around. You've reached Greece in the 5th century B.C. It's a time when the country is split into a lot of small city-states, each ruling small areas. Some of these city-states have formed leagues and friendships. But others are constantly fighting. The two most powerful city-states — Athens and Sparta — are often at war to determine who will rule Greece. Despite all the fighting, tremendous advances in science, art, and philosophy are being made.

The Chronoskimmer's computer beeps, letting you know it's found some leads.

If you want to question:

Socrates — go to #128

Plato — go to #7

Aristotle — go to #86

If you think the crook traveled to:

12th century Japan — go to #40

16th century Mexico — go to #165

14th century China — go to #53

#20. You've tracked Lotta Style to the public baths. The Romans used the baths not only as a place for bathing, but also as a gym and a gambling casino! There's a lot of noise and activity, but you don't find one trace of Lotta. There's not a lot to learn, so you'd better go to #111.

#21. You've landed in 16th century Mexico. Hernán Cortés has taken over the Aztec capital, Tenochtitlán, and imprisoned the Aztec ruler, Montezuma. At the moment, Cortés is searching the city for hidden treasures. You interrupt him to ask about the crook you're trailing.

"She was here," Cortés tells you angrily. "She tried to steal some of my gold. And it's all mine!"

You don't point out that he's actually stealing it himself from the Aztecs. He's got a sword, and, well, you don't. Instead you ask Cortés if the thief said anything that might help you capture her.

Cortés isn't too interested. "She said something about having an outdoor hobby. And about going to Asia next. She can go to blazes for all I care!"

You leave Cortés to his brooding and head back to the Chronoskimmer at #105 to check on these clues.

#22. You've trailed Carl LaFong to a spot in England that will become known as Sherwood Forest. This is where Robin Hood will hide out in a hundred years or so. But right now all you can find is deer. Better get along to #111 to find out why you are in the wrong place.

#23. You've landed in Japan in the year 1185. Yoritomo Minamoto is one of the greatest soldiers in Japanese history. He has just managed to end centuries of civil war and unite the Japanese people. In

1192 he will proclaim himself shogun, or military ruler, and claim to be acting on behalf of the emperor. Actually, the emperor will do as Yoritomo tells him! You are allowed in to see Yoritomo only after you remove your shoes as a sign of respect. You ask him about the crook you're trailing.

"She was here," he tells you. "She mentioned something about going to a land to the west of us. I don't know why she'd bother. Only Japan is interesting."

You thank him for his help and return to your time machine at #40 to check out this clue.

#24. You've reached Samarkand, one of the oldest cities in the world. Samarkand is on the road to China from the Middle East. But you are totally lost! Better make your way to #72 right now!

#25. You've trailed B. B. D. O'Brien to Damascus. This city is already three thousand years old and famous for being the capital of Syria. It is also the place where some of the finest material in the world is produced. You might as well go shopping, since there's no trace of B. B. D. O'Brien here. Then, when you're done, find your way to #111 to find out what happens next.

#26. You've reached Japan in the 12th century, and you're in the mountains. Since almost everyone at this time lives on the coast or in the plains, there's nobody around. Give up and go to #72.

#27. The Chronoskimmer lands, and you find yourself in China in the 14th century. This is the start of the Ming Dynasty, which was one of the world's great powers. But at this time the Chinese have thrown off their foreign rulers — the Mongol Khans — and taken control of their own country again. It's a time of great culture and peace, and the Chinese rule almost all of the Far East.

The computer in the Chronoskimmer beeps. You read the printout to discover what people you should interrogate.

If you want to speak with:
Chang Chu-cheng — go to #31
Lung Ch'ing — go to #149
Anda — go to #107

#28. During the 5th century B.C., Cimon was a great Greek general. Unfortunately, he always seemed to choose the wrong side to support. At one time he was even expelled by his home city of Athens. Eventually his pupil Pericles came to power. Right now, though, Cimon is alone in his tent, sighing about all the battles he's won without actually winning a war. You ask him about the crook you're chasing.

"Oh, he was here," Cimon tells you. "A very dull person. He said he was going somewhere after this where he could talk to a famous writer. He didn't think I was worth talking to, I suppose." He looks at you. "I don't suppose you'd want to hear about my campaigns, would you?"

"Some other time," you tell him. "I'm in a bit of a rush right now."

"That's what they all say," complains Cimon, and returns to sulking. You get out quickly and head for your Chronoskimmer at #79 to check on the clue he gave you.

#29. You've landed in West Africa in the 19th century. It's a time of great changes. European explorers are busy making maps of the countries they find, while the local people are forming empires of their own. The Muslim people are using their religion to unify the countries they conquer, while European missionaries are spreading Christianity. It's a mixture that doesn't work too well, and you know that it will still be a problem in the 20th century.

The computer beeps to let you know it's found information for you. ☞

If you want to talk to:

Usman dan Fodio — *go to #109*
Ar-Haj 'Umar — *go to #13*
The Muslim priest — *go to #38*

If you think that the crook's gone on to:

5th century B.C. Greece — *go to #84*
11th century England — *go to #147*
12th century Japan — *go to #51*

#30. You've arrived in Rome in 48 B.C., to find General Pompey, a great Roman soldier. He defeated Spartacus, an escaped slave. He also won great victories in the Middle East. For a time he was a ruling partner in Rome with Julius Caesar, but then he opposed Caesar's plans to seize power and was soon chased out of Rome. A few months later he was assassinated in Africa.

Right now though, you find him in his tent so you ask him about the thief you're trailing.

"He was here," Pompey tells you. "A silly person. He said he was off to somewhere in Europe next. I told him I was planning a trip myself, as soon as I can get an army together. I'll beat that Caesar yet!"

You wish him luck even though you know he'll never get the chance. Then you head back to the Chronoskimmer at #77 to check your clue.

#31. Chang Chu-cheng turns out to be the secretary to the emperor. He's not like any secretary you've ever known, though — he's actually responsible for seeing that the emperor's orders are carried out. Chang is virtually running the whole empire himself and is a very powerful man. You ask him about the crook you're chasing.

"I'm very sorry," he tells you, "but I know nothing about the person you seek." He waves a hand toward his overflowing desk. "I have so much work to do, I rarely see visitors."

You can sympathize with him: Your own desk looks almost as messy. You thank him anyway and head back to your time machine at #27 to follow another lead.

#32. The Chronoskimmer has brought you to China in the 14th century. The Great Wall of China has been finished, and you're standing on the wrong side of it. Better get a move on to #72 and find out what happened.

#33. You find Euripides in 5th-century Greece, and is he grumpy! As a result, he's not too well liked in Athens. After he dies, however, he'll be declared a genius. Right now he's mostly called an old grouch.

You ask him about the crook you're trailing.

"Her?" he says, with a sniff. "What a horrible woman. All she could talk about was wanting some foreign food. What's wrong with the food here, I ask you? Some people are never satisfied, are they? I told her that if she didn't like it here, she should go somewhere else. She said she was off to a Muslim country. Good riddance. Now, what about you? Do you want to read my latest play?"

You apologize and tell him you've got to be off, too. He frowns at you and returns to his work. You head back to the Chronoskimmer at #84 to check out the clues he's given you.

#34. Your Chronoskimmer carries you back through time to the coast of England in the 11th century. In this period, England is mostly a lot of warring factions loosely ruled by Edward the Confessor. He's a very holy man, but not a good king. The king's armies don't have enough weapons, and are not very efficient, and he doesn't like fighting very much.

The Chronoskimmer's computer beeps to tell you that it's finished scanning the area. It has discovered that the crook you're trailing spoke to three people. There are also three possible places where the thief may have gone. If you talk to witnesses, they may be able to help you narrow down where the crook has fled.

If you want to talk to:
Harold Hardrada — go to #126
King Harold — go to #89
Tostig — go to #151

If you think that the crook has gone to:
12th century Japan — go to #42
1st century Rome B.C. — go to #71
16th century Mexico — go to #105

#35. You've landed in England in the 11th century, in the town of Whitby. Viking raiders are burning down the town, so you'd better get out of here fast! Take a quick trip to #72!

#36. You've landed in Mexico in the 16th century. The Spanish conquistadors — the soldiers of fortune — are hunting everywhere for gold. They don't like the way you look, so they start firing their muskets. Luckily, they miss, so you've got time to flee to #72.

#37. You've tracked Alexander Graham Edison to a Roman arena. The Romans like sports, especially when they're violent. Personally, you think it's very sick.

As you arrive, the lions are let loose. You push your way to the front of the crowd and realize that the lions are chasing Edison around the ring. If you don't save him, he's going to be their supper tonight!

Luckily, you stopped at the pet store on your way to work this morning and bought some cat-nip for your own kitten. Hoping it works just as well with big cats as with small ones, you throw it into the ring.

Immediately the lions start purring and rolling over to have their tummies tickled. You help Alexander Graham Edison out of the ring. He falls on his knees and starts kissing your feet in gratitude. You ask him to stop it. "You're under arrest," you tell him. "It's back to jail for you."

As the police haul him away, he tells you where he's hidden the stolen Aztec temple. You immediately call the Chief and inform him.

"Terrific work, detective," the Chief says happily. "You'd better add up your travel points and head to the back of the book to see if you've earned that promotion!"

#38. You find the Muslim priest or mullah at prayer and wait till he's finished. In the Islamic faith, everyone must kneel facing the holy city of Mecca to pray several times a day. When the mullah is done, you ask him about the crook you're chasing.

"That scoundrel!" the mullah cries. "I asked her if she observes the holy fasts, and she told me that she only watches TV — whatever that is! I told her to be gone from here, and she said she was on her way to Europe. Good riddance, if you ask me."

You thank him for his help and hurry back to the Chronoskimmer at #29 to check out the clues he's given you.

#39. You've traced Lotta Style to the Abbey of Battle. William the Conqueror built the abbey on the battlefield where he defeated and killed King Harold. William is still very sad that he had to fight the battle to get the crown. But he felt that the crown was his right. You feel very sad because there's no sign of Lotta here. You'd better get along to #111 to find out the reason.

#40. The Chronoskimmer sets you down in 12th-century Japan. It is a country made up of four major islands — Hokkaido, Honshu, Shikoku, and Kyushu — and almost 3,500 much smaller islands. It's a very beautiful country, even though there are plenty of live volcanoes and many earthquakes. The country has just become united under the first military ruler, Yoritomo, who is known as the shogun.

The computer beeps to let you know it's finished gathering leads for you to follow.

If you want to interview:

Yoritomo — go to #23

Yoshitsune — go to #95

Benkei — go to #69

If you think that the crook went to:

19th century West Africa — go to #145

16th century Mexico — go to #120

8th–12th-century Islamic World — go to #11

#41. You've landed in 12th-century Japan. The Hojo family live in a heavily guarded fortress. They are rivals of the ruling shogun, and in less than forty years they will come to power. Right now, though, they are simply biding their time. Tokimasa, the Hojo family leader, greets you with kindness. You ask him about the crook you're after.

"He was here," Tokimasa tells you. "We offered him a meal, but he did not like our sushi. He said he prefers his food to be very spicy. When I asked him where he was going next, he said to meet a tribe called the Fulani."

You thank Tokimasa for his help. He offers you some sushi as well. You discover that it's raw fish! "I'd rather have a hamburger and fries," you confess.

Then you head back to your time machine at #158 to check out these latest clues.

#42. You've reached Japan in the 12th century. You find yourself in an area overrun by warrior monks, who are terrorizing the local people. You are forced to make a quick escape to #72.

#43. Livy is hard at work in his study when you arrive in Rome in the 1st century B.C. He's been working on his huge *History of Rome* and has ink all over his fingers. "A visitor," he says, with a smile. "I've been dying for an excuse to take a rest." He waves his hand over the scroll of parchment he's working on. "I'm on book 100," he says proudly. "Only another 42 to go."

"You'll take up a library all by yourself," you reply.

"It is my life's work," he tells you. "The Emperor Augustus has given it his highest blessing. He's very pleased with it. Now, how can I help you?"

You explain about the crook you're looking for. "I've not seen him myself," Livy answers. "But I have a report here somewhere. . . ." He pokes about in a box filled with research notes. "Ah, here we are! Yes, one of my friends spoke to the thief. The man said he was going next to see a city that's built in a lake. That's right — I thought it was most unusual."

You thank him for his help and leave him to his writing. You head back to your time machine at #168 to check out this new clue.

#44. You've trailed Benjamin Hama to a Chinese restaurant. Inside, you're handed a fortune cookie. When you break it open, there's a slip of paper. It reads: *Head straight to #111*. Better do as it says!

#45. The Chronoskimmer lands you in Rome in the 1st century B.C. Everyone's at the games, so there's nobody for you to question. Better head for #72 and find out why you are in the wrong place.

#46. You've trailed Alexander Graham Edison to a used-camel market in Baghdad. It's the wrong place and the wrong time. The only one who will talk to you is a salesman. He tries to sell you a camel that a little old lady used just to go to the mosque on Fridays. The only way to get away from the annoying man is to head for #111.

#47. Xicatenga is one of the chiefs who became friendly with the Spanish. Like a lot of his fellow chiefs, he hates the cruel and greedy Aztecs and is happy to side with someone who might just break their power. He's more than happy to talk to you, so you ask about the crook you're trailing.

"I saw him," Xicatenga tells you. "The brown-haired one was trying to steal gold. I had my men throw him out of my village. He shook his fist at them and said he was going somewhere in the Near East where he'd be better treated."

You thank him for his help and go back to your Chronoskimmer at #52 to check out this clue.

#48. Adama is the emir, or ruler, of an area he's named after himself, Adamawa, in West Africa. He's been a very successful general and rules quite a lot of the local tribes. He greets you when you arrive, and you ask him about the woman you're chasing.

"Yes, I spoke to her," he replies. "She loves dogs, as do I, and we had a lot of fun talking about them. Do you like dogs?"

"Love them," you tell him. "Especially bloodhounds. I could use one right now. Did she say where she was going?"

"Only that it was in the Far East," he replies.

You thank him for his help and head back to your

time machine at #145 to check out these new clues.

#49. In 1st-century B.C. Rome, Cicero is a very famous politician and speaker. You find him at home when you arrive. He's tired out from his campaigns to restore democracy to Rome. Marc Antony will have him killed in the near future to shut him up, but right now he's full of energy. The only problem is that after all his campaigning and public speaking, he's lost his voice and can't talk to you! So you have to go back to #146 and try another lead.

#50. The Chronoskimmer carries you back through time, and when you emerge, you are in China in the 14th century. It's a time of great learning and prosperity. The Chinese emperors have explored and conquered much of Asia. They're trading with Europe, and the whole country is filled with enthusiasm. It's a very busy place, and it looks as if it could be fun here — if you had the time just to sightsee!

The Chronoskimmer's computer beeps to let you know it has some information. It's been scanning the area and has found out that the crook who stole the Ming vase spoke to three people. The thief then fled to some other time and country. If you talk to

the witnesses, they may be able to help you decide
where the thief went.

If you want to speak to:
Hung Wu — go to #64
Cheng-Zi — go to #136
Yung Lo — go to #81

If you think the crook fled to:
12th century Japan — go to #26
8th–12th century Islamic world — go to #98
1st century B.C. Rome — go to #168

#51. You've landed on a small island óff the coast
of Japan in the 12th century. The only living things
here are cormorants, birds that dive for fish. You'd better go on to #72 and find out what the catch is!

#52. You've landed in Mexico in the 16th century.
The Aztecs have conquered almost all of Mexico, and
they're very unpopular. Not only do they take all the
gold from the tribes they conquer, but they also take
human captives. These prisoners are then sacrificed
to the Aztecs' bloodthirsty gods. As a result, many of
the tribes decide to team up with the recently arrived
Spanish invaders to fight the Aztecs. They feel that
nobody could be as cruel as the Aztecs.

The computer in your Chronoskimmer beeps to

let you know it's found some leads for you to follow.

If you want to meet:

Diego Velásquez — go to #106

Xicatenga — go to #47

Guatemoc — go to #68

If you think the crook went to:

8th-12th century Islamic world — go to #6

19th century West Africa — go to #90

12th century Japan — go to #156

#53. The Chronoskimmer lands you in China in the 14th century. There are agents of the secret police all about. You're afraid they'll steal your time machine, so you're forced to flee to #72.

#54. You've landed in 16th-century Mexico. You find Cuitlahautzin in the council chambers of the city Tenochtitlán. He's the brother of Montezuma II and will become the new ruler when his brother dies. He's a very worried man right now, but he agrees to take the time to talk to you. You ask about the crook you're looking for.

"He was here," he tells you. "He mentioned something about meeting a samurai, whatever that is."

You thank him for his help and head back to your Chronoskimmer at #130 to check out this fresh clue.

#55. Eisai is a Buddhist monk who introduced a new form of the faith to Japan, called Rinzai Zen. He's meditating when you arrive. Eisai believes that this is the way to discover the truth. When you are shown in, Eisai rises and greets you. "How may I be of service?" he asks politely. You explain about the crook you're chasing.

"She was here," Eisai tells you. "I tried to get her to meditate, but she said she wasn't interested. I told her that the only free person is the thinking person. All others are slaves to fear and ignorance. She said she was going to a land where they had already freed slaves."

You thank him for his help. "Would you like to meditate?" he asks. "It's very relaxing."

"I can't relax till I've caught this thief," you reply. You head back to your Chronoskimmer at #135 to check out this new clue.

#56. You've tracked Sarah Nade to Exeter. This is an old Roman town, and you've been roaming about too long. Time to head for #111 to see what's up.

#57. Wang Chen is the powerful state administrator of the Ming emperor. He's also very much in trouble right now. Because of his bad advice, the

Ming army was beaten by an army led by Yesen, and the emperor was taken prisoner. As a result of all this, Wang Chen is in jail, waiting to be executed. He's not allowed any visitors, and the guards insist that you leave. You head back to your time machine at #141 to check out another lead. Let's hope you have more luck next time!

#58. You've landed in England in the 11th century. There are roving bands of thieves about called "wolfsheads," and they're outlaws who rob and kill. To avoid being caught by one of these gangs, you have to head straight to #72.

#59. You find Scheherazade in her luxurious room in the palace. She's composing the latest of her stories, which she uses to keep her husband amused. She is a very intelligent and nice lady, and you can't help but like her. You also can't help noticing that one of the servant girls is helping herself to some of Scheherazade's jewels.

Quickly you snatch up a rope of pearls and use it as a lasso to catch the crook. The girl struggles, and bits of stolen jewelry drop out of her pockets. Scheherazade is furious with the girl but delighted with you. She searches the girl and finds lots of other jewels. "And she's even taken a page from my latest story!" cries Scheherazade. Then she looks at the page. "No, this isn't mine. Do you know what it is?"

You look at the page in delight: It's a list of all the escaped members of Carmen's gang and where they're hiding out!

If you think the thief who stole the Viking longboat is:

B. B. D. O'Brien — go to #25
Alexander Graham Edison — go to #46
Sarah Nade — go to #131
Chips Motherboard — go to #97
Benjamin Hama — go to #63
Li Non Mee — go to #167
Lotta Style — go to #9
Carl LaFong — go to #80

#60. Saladin is a powerful general *and* all-around nice guy. He's happy to see you and offers you Turkish delight while you talk. His real name is Salah al-Din, but the crusaders from Europe call him Saladin, which is easier to pronounce. He's the Sultan of Egypt and has fought and beaten the crusaders in Jerusalem a number of times. He's almost as well known for being generous and kind as he is for being a soldier. You ask him about the crook you're hunting.

"That man was here," he tells you. "He was trying

to steal some of the loot we took in our last battle. He was lucky to escape before I could have his hands chopped off! He said something about fleeing a thousand years or so into the past. I told him his brains were fried. He said that he doesn't eat fried food—he prefers everything microwaved. What does that mean? Is it of any help?"

"A lot of help," you say. Wishing him luck, you head back to your Chronoskimmer, located at #6, to follow up these new leads.

#61. You've tracked B. B. D. O'Brien to a seafood house in Canton, China. There's plenty of squid, scallops, and lobster on the menu, but there's no sign of B. B. D. O'Brien. After you stay for a meal, you'd better pack up and head for #111.

#62. The Chronoskimmer has brought you to West Africa in the 19th century. It's a very rich area that exports great quantities of oil and agricultural products. In the 19th century it's also an area that many people are seeking to control. The Portuguese controlled parts of the area for hundreds of years, but Muslim chiefs are conquering large portions of the territory in holy wars called jihads.

The computer beeps to tell you it has found some

leads for you to follow.

If you want to talk to:
Osei Tutu — go to #70
Okomfo Anokye — go to #108
Kokofu — go to #150

If you think that the thief fled to:
11th century England — go to #12
1st century Rome — go to #45
16th century Mexico — go to #138

#63. You've tracked Benjamin Hama to a mosque in Baghdad. The mosque is a Muslim gathering place for worship, and must have a large tower where the muezzin can call the faithful to prayer. You're getting a call, too, but it's to go to #111 immediately.

#64. Hung Wu is the first emperor of the Ming (which means "Bright") Dynasty. His real name was Chu Yüan-Chang, but he adopted the name of Hung Wu when he became emperor. He also had a third name, T'ai Tsu, which was used only on religious occasions. Hung Wu is a very colorful character, with many interests and passions. He agrees to talk to you, so you ask about the thief you're chasing.

"He took the Ming vase," the emperor tells you.

"My men heard him say he was going to visit the writer of a famous book about war."

You thank him and wish him a glorious reign. Then you head back to your Chronoskimmer at #50 to check out this clue.

#65. You've landed in Japan in the 12th century. Unfortunately, you've arrived right on the top of Mount Fuji, which is a volcano in the middle of erupting. You'd better flee to #72 right away.

#66. You've managed to follow Carl LaFong's trail to a Roman forum. It's the Roman equivalent of a shopping mall that's filled with people selling all kinds of things. It's so crowded that even if Carl is here, you'll never find him. Better head to #111.

#67. Bernal Díaz is a quiet, thoughtful man. He's making notes of everything that happens on his journey into Mexico. When he's an old man, he'll write a fascinating and moving book called *The Conquest of New Spain* about his adventures. He's got an eye for detail, so you really hope he can help you. You ask him about the thief you're chasing.

"She was here for a while," he tells you. "I spoke

with her. She mentioned how much she loves the outdoors. Her hobby is something connected with being outside, I gather. And she mentioned that she was going to a place where she could read a book in its original language about a fellow called Genji."

You thank him for his help and rush back to your time machine at #105 to check out this lead.

#68. You find Guatemoc preparing to attack the Spanish invaders. He's a nephew of the Emperor Montezuma II, and a fierce warrior. You ask about the thief you're after.

"He of the brown hair?" asks Guatemoc. "He was here. He said he was going east of Mexico on his next trip. He was trying to steal some of our gold, I had my men kick him out."

You hurry back to the Chronoskimmer at #52 to check up on these clues.

#69. You find Benkei cleaning the swords of his master, Yoshitsune, in his room. They will become famous in future ages as the greatest warrior and servant of their age. Together they will flee the corrupt reign of Yoshitsune's brother Yoritomo. At the moment, Benkei is getting ready for their escape. He has only a few moments to talk with you as he packs. You ask about the thief you're chasing.

"She came by here," Benkei tells you. "She spoke of going forward in time from here. I do not know what she meant, but I hope that this will help you."

You thank him and wish him luck, then head back to the Chronoskimmer, located at #40, to check out this clue.

#70. In 19th-century West Africa, Osei Tutu is the great leader of the Ashanti tribe. He has conquered land in what you now know as the country of Ghana. A firm believer in symbols, Osei Tutu claimed divine leadership for his rule and created the Golden Stool. Tutu claimed the stool descended from heaven, and all future rulers would be expected to sit on it. Osei Tutu knew that people like to see symbols of power. He's a very clever and interesting man and agrees to talk to you about the crook you're chasing.

"A wise ruler allows no criminals in his country," he tells you. "As soon as we discovered that the man you're chasing was here, I ordered my men to throw him out. He left saying he was off to see a nicer king named Edward. I hope this Edward throws him out, too."

"I hope he throws him in jail," you reply. "It'll make my job easier." You thank the king for his help and return to your time machine at #62 to check out this clue.

#71. You've landed in Rome in the 1st century B.C. A soldier salutes you and hands you a note. It's from the Chief, ordering you to head straight to #72.

#72. You've fallen for one of the gang's tricks! Somehow you've followed the wrong clue to this spot. You'd better go back to the time and place where you landed and check your clues again. This isn't where you're supposed to be. You did remember to leave your bookmark in the right place to go back to, didn't you? Better luck next time!

#73. You've tracked Li Non Mee to Hadrian's Wall in the North of England. This wall was built here to stop invaders. Now it's deserted. If you want to find anyone, you'll have to go to #111.

#74. Ibn Rushd is a great philosopher in the time of 12th-century Islam. He is better known in Europe, however, as Averroës. Ibn Rushd became famous as a writer on the Greek philosophers, and he is considered a great man. He's also very quiet and polite and is happy to talk to you. You ask him about the stolen manuscript.

"A great tragedy," he tells you. "But I hope that

you can recover the book. All I can tell you is that the thief mentioned wanting to see a Great Wall."

"It's a great help," you tell him and hurry back to your Chronoskimmer at #88 to check out the clue.

#75. Montezuma II is the regal ruler of the Aztecs. Once a very powerful man, he's now trapped between the army of the Spanish invaders and his own soldiers. His own men would sooner see him dead than used as a puppet of the invaders, so they are going to kill him very soon. Right now, though, he agrees to see you, even though he's very glum.

"This is a bad time for my people," he tells you. "The theft of the temple only makes this matter worse. You must track down the thief and return the temple to my people."

You ask if he has any clues. "Only that the villain spoke about meeting a samurai," he tells you. "I don't know what that is, but I hope you do."

"I'll check it out," you promise and head right back to your time machine at #130.

#76. In 5th-century Greece, Aeschylus is known as one of the great playwrights of Greek history. He's particularly fond of writing tragedies that tell of the rich and powerful who become too arrogant and ignore the gods. He's a very good writer but gets terribly depressed. He's very unhappy when you meet him. You try to cheer him up by telling him a few jokes, but it's no use. He doesn't even crack a smile. He simply sighs. You're getting nowhere with him, so you head back to the Chronoskimmer at #84 to try a different lead.

#77. The Chronoskimmer lands you in Rome in the 1st century B.C. It's a time of great change. The general Julius Caesar has led his troops across the Rubicon River and into Rome to seize power. Many people hate him for this, which will lead to his being assassinated in a few years' time. Till then he'll rule most of the Roman world with a fist of steel. Many of the citizens are happy enough, because this is the start of an age of wealth for the city.

The computer beeps, letting you know it's found some clues.

If you want to talk to:
Julius Caesar — go to #18
Pompey — go to #30
Crassus — go to #144

If you think the thief fled to:

☞

16th century Mexico — go to #94
11th century England — go to #110
5th century B.C. Greece — go to #132

#78. You've traced Li Non Mee to a pottery factory. This is where the expensive and valuable Ming vases are produced. She's obviously here to steal one! You creep inside and see that she's holding up the poor people producing the pots. You think quickly. Scooping up some of the clay that's used in the factory, you slip up behind her. Then you slap the clay over her eyes, blinding her.

"I can't see!" she yells. You karate-chop the gun from her hand.

"Don't worry," you tell her. "I'll make sure you get to jail safely." You reach into her coat and find the stolen manuscript of *The Rubáiyát* in her pocket. "And I'll see that this is returned to Omar Khayyám." With a grin, you recite:

"A book of verses underneath the bough,
A jug of water, a loaf of bread — and Thou
With this book tucked inside your coat
Are off to a jail cell right now."

You call up the Chief and tell him you've captured Li Non Mee and recovered the stolen book. He's really pleased with you.

"Well done indeed!" he says. "Well, better add up your travel points and head for the back of the book to see if you've earned that promotion and a bonus!"

#79. The Chronoskimmer has landed you in Greece during the 5th century B.C. This is probably the highest point in all of Greek history. The great buildings like the Parthenon in Athens will be built. Great books and plays will be written, wise philosophers and great generals will live. It's a very exciting time to visit, and you only wish you had the time to look around. So much is happening here!

The Chronoskimmer's computer beeps, reminding you that you've got a job to do. It's found some leads for you to follow.

If you want to speak to:

Cimon — go to #28

Pericles — go to #4

Brasidas — go to #121

If you think the crook went to:

1st century B.C. Rome — go to #146

11th century England — go to #58

12th century Japan — go to #96

#80. You've traced Carl LaFong to the desert. A lot of monks come here to pray and to try to see God. There's no food or water, and it's very hot. Since you don't want to work on your tan, you'd better head straight for #111.

#81. Yung Lo is the uncle of Cheng Zi. When Cheng-Zi comes to power and changes his name to Emperor Hung Wu, his bad decisions will stir up trouble. Yung Lo will then seize power and become the third Ming emperor. He is a strong and capable man, unlike his nephew. As he plans his strategy, he agrees to talk to you.

"I saw the man who took the vase," he tells you. "An

odd person who mentioned something about traveling back in time more than a thousand years."

You thank him for his help. Then you head back to the Chronoskimmer at #50 to check out this clue.

#82. You've arrived in Mexico during the 16th century. The Aztecs have conquered most of the country. Their armies are out taking captives for human sacrifices. Unless you want to become one, you'd better head straight to #72.

#83. The monk Honen was one of the founders of "Pure Land" Buddhism. Unlike many monks, he believed that Buddhism was meant for everyone, not just monks. He was certain that all could become a part of the faith if they only believed and wanted to be saved. He is a man who will talk to anyone, so he's quite happy to talk to you. You ask him about the crook you're after.

"That one was here," he replies. "I told him to give up his ways and become a monk. I offered him a bowl of rice, but he said that he likes his food spicy. He was not interested in Buddhism and said he was going to where there are Muslims, followers of a faith called Islam."

You thank him for his help and politely turn down

his offer of a bowl of rice. "I like mine fried, with chop suey from my local Chinese takeout," you reply. Then you head back to your time machine at #158 to check up on these clues.

#84. Your Chronoskimmer has landed you in Greece in the 5th century B.C. The country is made up of many small city-states who join in uneasy alliances. They are facing invasions by the greatest power of their day, that of Persia. Darius and Xerxes will both send huge armies to invade Greece. But the Greeks will hold these armies at bay, winning great victories.

Right now things are pretty quiet, until your onboard computer beeps. It's uncovered some leads for you to follow.

If you want to question:
Aeschylus — go to #76
Sophocles — go to #155
Euripides — go to #33

If you think the thief went to:
8th–12th century Islamic world — go to #17
19th century West Africa — go to #118
11th century England — go to #93

#85. When you land in 1st century, Rome, you find Virgil on the small farm he owns outside the city. He's one of Rome's greatest poets, but he loves farm life above everything else. He uses it as background for his poems. Right now he's working on his masterpiece, *The Aeneid*. This tells the story of the fall of Troy and the wanderings and adventures of Aeneas, a prince of the city, who later founded Rome. He takes a break to talk to you.

"Yes," he tells you, "I saw the man you're after. He told me that he didn't much like Rome and was going to a country that lies to the west." He offers you a glass of milk. "I milked the cow myself," he says proudly. You compliment him on his skills, then head back to your Chronoskimmer at #168 to check out the clue he's given you.

#86. Aristotle is one of Plato's students, in ancient Greece. Aristotle is the son of a doctor, and one day he'll become famous as a philosopher, too. He'll also be the teacher of Alexander the Great — the young man who will conquer most of the then-known world.

Aristotle is interested in how things work — from science to politics to human nature. He's endlessly interested in everything, and it's hard to have a straight chat with him about the thief you're chasing.

"She had brown eyes," he tells you. "Don't you find eye colors fascinating? I wonder why hers should be brown and mine are blue-gray?"

"Did she say where she was going?" you ask, not wanting to get into a long discussion.

"Oh, she said something about going to a time before the Ming Dynasty came to power. Don't you think politics is interesting? Why should one country be ruled by an emperor, do you think, and another by a president?"

"It takes all kinds to make a world," you tell him.

"That's very good," he says, making a note of it. "I like the sound of that. But all kinds of what, I wonder? And how many worlds are there?"

You hurry out before you go crazy, and head back to your time machine at #19 to check out the clues he's given you.

#87. You've trailed Chips Motherboard to the catacombs under Rome. These are long passageways under the city in which the bodies of the dead are buried. It's very spooky down here, and you're not happy. You're even less happy when there's no sign of Chips — dead or alive — and you quickly head back to #111.

#88. The Chronoskimmer lands you in Baghdad, the capital of the Islamic world of this time. For several hundred years — the 8th to 12th centuries — the Arab nations are becoming united under the new religion of Islam. United by this faith, soldiers and mullahs or priests will spread the Islamic word from Africa to the farthest reaches of Asia. They will even invade Spain and other parts of Europe.

Right now, though, Baghdad is a city bustling with traders and explorers, students and writers, scientists and rulers. The computer that's built into your time machine beeps and then spits out a piece of paper. It's been scanning the area and discovered that the thief who stole *The Rubáiyát* was seen by three people before fleeing to another time and place. If you question these people, you might be able to discover where the crook fled to.

If you want to speak to:
Omar Khayyám — go to #137
Ibn Rushd — go to #74
Ibn Sina — go to #153

If you think the crook went to:
16th century Mexico — go to #99
14th century China — go to #141
12th century Japan — go to #15

#89. It's 11th century England, and King Edward has died and Harold has come to the throne. Right now, Harold's marching north with his men. A huge Viking army has landed in England, and Harold is going to fight them. The battle will take place at Stamford Bridge, and Harold will win brilliantly. The problem is that almost immediately afterward William will land his forces in the south. Harold will march back to fight him, but his tired men will lose the battle, and Harold will be killed. Right now, Harold is in good spirits and confident he'll win the upcoming battle. You ask him about the crook you're looking for.

"I saw her when she took the ship," he tells you. "Big deal. One less Viking ship is fine by me."

"Did she say anything when you saw her?" you ask.

"Only some nonsense about going forward in time." Harold smiles grimly. "Well, my men are going forward, too — but into battle."

You wish him luck, then head off to your time machine at #34 to see where the crook may be heading.

#90. You've reached West Africa in the 19th century. There are huge herds of wildlife here to see, which is great — except there's no sign of the crook you're after. Once you've had your fill of watching the wildlife, you'd better head along to #72.

#91. You've trailed Lotta Style to the Great Wall of China. It's just been finished and will help defend the country's borders. You're finished, too, but you haven't captured Lotta. You'd better head for #111 to find out why you're in the wrong place.

#92. You arrive at Westminster Abbey, in London. It's one of the most famous churches in all of England, and was founded by King Edward in 1065. Edward's a very religious man and will be known to history as Edward the Confessor. But he's not really a very smart king. He can't make up his mind who he wants to be king when he dies. He doesn't have any children of his own, and he keeps switching favorites. Speaking of switching subjects, you ask him about the crook you're chasing.

"I saw him," Edward confesses. "A brown-haired man. He mentioned that he was off to a country to the east of England." A bell rings. "Sorry," the king tells you. "Time for prayers. Must be off."

"Say one for me," you tell him. "I'm going to need all the help I can get." Then you head back to your time machine at #12 to check out the clue he's given you.

#93. The Chronoskimmer lands you in England in the 11th century. There are Norman soldiers about, but they speak only French, so you can't get anyone to answer your questions. You'd better head straight to #72.

#94. You've arrived in Mexico in the 16th century, but you're deep in the jungle here. It's almost impossible to get around because the foliage is so thick and overgrown. You have to pack it in and head for #72 instead.

#95. You find Yoshitsune getting ready for a trip. He and his brother, Yoritomo, have had a major argument. Yoritomo is the shogun, or military ruler, and he thinks Yoshitsune is trying to seize his power. He's going to have Yoshitsune hunted down very soon. But the famous warrior is a gentle and polite man when not worried about his brother, so he agrees to talk with you before he leaves.

"I saw the woman you seek," he tells you. "She said she admired great warriors and had always wanted to meet me. She was going to meet another great warrior who will not be born yet for hundreds of years."

You wish him luck and head back to your time machine (#40) to check out this clue.

#96. You've arrived in Japan in the 12th century. It's very pretty with the cherry blossoms in bloom, but that's all there is here for you to see. You'd better take a quick trip to #72 to see why you are in the wrong place.

#97. You've followed a tip that the thief, Chips Motherboard, is in Morocco, a country at the tip of Africa. Unfortunately, your tip is not a tiptop tip. Chip's skipped. You'd better take a trip to #111.

#98. The Chronoskimmer lands you in the Islamic world. Everyone here speaks Arabic, and nobody understands what you're talking about. You'd better move on to #72 to find out why you're in the wrong place.

#99. You land in Mexico in the 16th century. The trouble is that there's plague about. Many of the natives will die from diseases brought over from Europe by the Spanish invaders. You'll catch no crooks here, only germs. Better pack up and flee to #72 right away.

#100. You find Queen Edith in her room, having her long hair combed by her maid. It's 11th-century

England, and Edith is the daughter of Earl Godwin and wife of King Edward. Her brother Harold is going to be the next king, but he'll have a very short reign. You ask Edith about the crook you're trailing.

"I saw him," she tells you. "He spoke about going to a place where he could meet a famous scientist and philosopher."

Thanking her for her help, you head back to your time machine at #12 to check out this clue.

#101. You've landed in 16th century Mexico. The Spanish invaders are all out looking for gold, so there's nobody to question. You'd better go to #72.

#102. You've trailed Chips Motherboard to Canterbury, England, sometime around the year 1050. This is a busy town that will become famous as the setting for *The Canterbury Tales*, one of the great books of English literature. Right now, though, it's a market town with a cathedral that's one of the most impressive in all England. Chips is in the cathedral, trying to steal the collection plate and all the money.

You tiptoe up behind him, and as he turns to run, you trip him. He falls into the font containing holy water. "Chips and dip," you joke. You pull him out before he drowns.

"Okay," you tell him. "Chips, you're under arrest for

stealing a Ming vase. It's back to Sing Sing for you."
You find the vase hidden in Chips's time machine.
Then you call the Chief to let him know you've cracked
the case — but not the vase!

"Very well done, detective," the Chief congratu-
lates you. "Well, you'd better add up your travel
points and head for the back of the book to see if
you've earned that promotion and bonus!"

#103. T'ien Shun is a Ming emperor who was held captive by foreign invaders for years before finally being set free. You are allowed by the guards to talk to him even though he's very depressed. After hearing what's been stolen, he agrees to tell you what he knows about the thief you're after.

"She came to see me a little while ago," T'ien Shun says. "She told me that she was going on to a country in Europe next."

You thank him for his help and wish him luck. Then you head back to your Chronoskimmer at #141 to check this clue out.

#104. You've followed B. B. D. O'Brien's trail to the Tiber River. Rome is built on seven hills, and the Tiber runs through it. You'd better run, too — to #111.

#105. The Chronoskimmer comes to a halt, and you're in Mexico in the 16th century. The Aztecs rule the country right now, but there have been other ruling tribes. Notable among these were the Olmecs and the Toltecs. The Olmecs built huge stone heads that still stand, some forty feet tall. The Toltecs built large, impressive cities. Both of them were finally succeeded by the Aztecs. The Aztecs in turn were defeated by the Spanish invaders under Cortés.

The computer beeps to let you know it's finished scanning for leads. You examine the print-out.

If you want to question:

Hernán Cortés — *go to #21*

Bernal Díaz — *go to #67*

Martín Cortés — *go to #159*

If you think the thief went to:

19th century West Africa — *go to #5*

14th century China — *go to #114*

12th century Japan — *go to #135*

#106. It's the 16th century, and you find Diego Velásquez, the Spanish ruler of the island of Cuba. Señor Velásquez sent Hernán Cortés to Mexico. Later, though, he became suspicious of Cortés and tried to have him recalled and put on trial. Velazquez was constantly trying to get Cortés into trouble. When you arrive, you find Velazquez looking over all his notes and letters on Cortés. When you explain that you're chasing a crook, he cheers up.

"I hate crooks," he tells you. "Cortés is a crook! I hate him. And this crook you're after — yes, I saw him. He tried to steal some of my gold, but he managed to escape when I tried to arrest him. One of the men told me the crook said he was going to a time after a book about Genji was written."

You thank him for his help and leave quickly. He might change his mind about you and have you thrown into his jail! You hurry back to your Chronoskimmer at #52 to check out your clue.

#107.   Anda is the warlord chief of a tribe called the Oirats. For almost thirty years he led his troops on raids into China. One time he almost sacked the capital city, Peking. Finally, though, he made peace and settled down. When you arrive, he's feeling happy that he can take a rest at last after all that fighting. He's so happy that he takes you into a special house he's built to hold all of his loot. When you enter, you see a man stuffing treasures into a sack.

Quickly you pick up a bag of gold coins and hurl it at the robber. It hits the man and stuns him. Anda calls in his guards, who drag the man away. On the floor where the thief fell down, you see a piece of paper. Opening it up, you smile with happiness. It's a list of all the places where Carmen's gang is hiding!

If you think *The Rubáiyát* was stolen by:

B. B. D. O'Brien — go to #61

Carl LaFong — go to #112

Sarah Nade — go to #157

Alexander Graham Edison — go to #3

Chips Motherboard — go to #133

Li Non Mee — go to #78

Lotta Style — go to #91
Benjamin Hama — go to #44

#108. Okomfo Anokye is a priest and the chief adviser to Osei Tutu, ruler of the Ashanti tribe in West Africa. It's the early 19th century, and it's a time of great ideas. Okomfo Anokye is the person who came up with many of the ideas the king has used to govern the tribe. You find Okomfo Anoky at home, deep in thought. He looks up and agrees to talk with you. You ask him about the crook you're after.

"I spoke with him," Okomfo tells you. "He said that he could travel through time and was going back less than a thousand years from now. If I had the power, I'd go forward in time to see what will become of my country."

"You'd like it," you reply. "I'm going back to the future when I catch this crook. Thanks for your help." You head back to your Chronoskimmer at #62 to check out this latest clue.

#109. The leader of the Fulani tribe, Usman dan Fodio, is a great warrior and planner. His men managed to conquer much of West Africa — a fertile and rich land that he ruled for many years during the 19th century. He's a wise and fascinating person. He greets you and listens as you explain your mission.

"The woman you're seeking was here," he tells you. "She spoke to me about some marvel called television that she likes to sit and watch. Myself, I like to sit and read the Koran, our holy book. Anyway, this woman you seek said she was going on from here to meet a very great writer."

You thank him for his help and head back to your time machine at #29 to follow up these clues.

#110. You've landed in 11th century England. The Normans have captured England under the leadership of William the Conqueror, but they are meeting a lot of resistance. There are many rebel forces, and the biggest one is hiding out right now in the marshes and fields around a town called Ely. The rebellion is being led by a man called Hereward the Wake, a famous soldier.

The computer beeps to let you know it's found out all it can. The crook seems to still be around in this time and has talked to three people.

If you want to talk to:

Hereward the Wake — go to #127
William the Conqueror — go to #14
Bishop Odo — go to #160

#111. Well, you've tracked the thief to the right destination — but you've made a mistake somewhere. You've tried to arrest the wrong person! Somewhere along the trail you've identified the wrong crook as the thief. You'd better head to the score chart to see how well you've done. **But because you've tried to capture the wrong person, add on ten extra travel points as a penalty.** Try this game again, but be a little more careful with your clues next time!

#112. You've trailed Carl LaFong to Szechwan Province. This is a populated area with its own special style of cooking. In your day, it's the spiciest sort of food on a Chinese restaurant's menu! But that's all the spice you'll find here, as there's no sign of Carl. Better hotfoot it to #111 to find out why.

#113. Ahuizotl is the old emperor of the Aztecs. Montezuma II is his nephew and will follow his uncle as ruler of the Aztecs. When you arrive, Ahuizotl is resting. He's an old man and can't talk for long. He listens as you explain your mission.

"I saw the thief from my window," he tells you. "As he passed by I heard him say something about reading the *Tales of the Heike* in its native language."

You thank him for his help and wish him well. Then you head back to your Chronoskimmer at #130 to check up on this lead.

#114. The Chronoskimmer lands you in China in the 14th century — right in the middle of the Gobi Desert. There's absolutely nothing but sand to be seen for miles. Since you don't have your tanning oil with you, there's nothing here to interest you. You head on to #72 instead.

#115. You've traced Alexander Graham Edison to York. This is a large town once ruled by the Vikings. It's an interesting town, but not for you — Edison isn't anywhere to be seen. You'd better go to #111 to find out why you are in the wrong place.

#116. Jajii Umar Tall is a 19th-century African warrior with skill and vision. He wants to unite the many tribes in West Africa under his own rule, and it looks as if he'll manage it, too. His troops are very brave, and they seem to be almost unstoppable. But he's stopped for a rest and agrees to chat with you. You ask him about the crook you're trailing.

"I saw her," he replies. "She said that on her next

trip she was going back in time five hundred years. She asked if I had any dogs, as she loves dogs. I told her that the only dogs about here are my enemies, who run from me like frightened puppies!"

You thank him for his help and return to the time machine at #145 to check out these clues.

#117. You find Marc Antony in his huge battle ship. It's powered by oars and sails and at the moment is moored in Egypt. Though he's supposed to be Octavian's partner in ruling the Roman world, Marc Antony is madly in love with the Egyptian queen, Cleopatra. He's joined forces with her to attack Octavian. You know that he'll be beaten in a huge sea battle. Both he and Cleopatra will commit suicide rather than be captured.

Right now, though, he's writing a love poem to Cleopatra. You can't get any sense out of him. All he wants you to do is to read his poems. They're all very mushy. One even begins: "Mama mia, I love Cleo"! Then you see something in the pile in a different handwriting. You start to read it and give a cry of triumph.

"You like that one?" asks Marc Antony.

"I love it," you say. It's not a poem, though — it's a list of the addresses where all of Carmen's gang members are hiding out!

If you think the Aztec temple was stolen by:

#118. The Chronoskimmer lands you in West Africa in the 19th century. There are a lot of soldiers moving about as the wars for control of the area heat up. But there's no sign of the crook you're after, so you'd better head for #72 to discover why you're in the wrong place.

#119. Nureddin is one of the warrior rulers of the Middle East during the 12th century. Together with Saladin, he has decided to drive the Christian soldiers from Europe out of Jerusalem and the Holy Land. A great fighter, he inspires his men in battle, and they rarely lose. At the moment, he's between fights and agrees to talk to you about the crook you're looking for.

"He was here," Nureddin tells you. "A silly man. He spoke about enjoying microwaves in his food. I told him that we have big waves in the sea off the coast. He got all upset and left. He said he was going to listen to somebody called Virgil."

You thank him for his help and then head back to the Chronoskimmer at #6 to follow up on these clues.

#120. The Chronoskimmer lands you in Mexico during the 16th century. The local people are all enjoying a cup of chocolate, their favorite drink. It's a bit too rich for you, though, but it's all you'll find here. When you've finished your chocolate, move on to #72.

#121. In 5th century Greece B.C. Brasidas was one of the greatest generals that the city-state of Sparta ever produced — and Sparta was noted for its soldiers. Unlike many of his fellow citizens, Brasidas was well liked and well spoken. His main fault was a refusal to come to peace with the city-state of Athens. His battles kept Greece in turmoil for years. Luckily, you've arrived while he's still planning his next fight, so he can take some time to answer your questions.

"I saw the scoundrel you're chasing," he tells you. "He mentioned going to a country in Europe."

You thank him for his help and leave him to his plans. Then you head back to your Chronoskimmer at #79 to check out this latest clue.

#122. The reign of Caliph Harūn ar-Rashid of Baghdad is remembered as the golden age of Islam. His power reached from North Africa to India, and under his rule many scholars and artists worked. He is famous for the stories told about him by Scheherazade, in *Thousand and One Nights.* You find him reading some of these stories, but he agrees to see you. You ask about the thief you're tailing.

"She came to see me," the caliph tells you. "She tried to steal some of Scheherazade's wonderful stories, so I had her thrown out of the city."

He can't tell you any more, so you head back to your Chronoskimmer at #17 to try a different lead.

#123. You've landed in Greece in the 5th century B.C. The Persian army has just invaded, and the local people have all fled. You'd better flee, too, to #72.

#124. Yesen is the military leader of the Mongol invaders who attacked Peking and captured Emperor T'ien Shun, during the 14th century in China. He's a brave but careful man, and he agrees to talk to you about the crook you're after.

"She came to me," he tells you. "She said something about being able to travel in time. She mentioned that her next trip would be almost two thousand years into the past. I didn't like her, and told her she'd be history if I saw her again."

You thank him for his help and head back to your time machine at #141 to check out this fresh clue.

#125.   You've trailed Li Non Mee to the temple of Mars, God of War. But the only people here are some Romans who have come to offer thanks for their victories in battle. You'd better head on to #111 right now.

#126.   Harold Hardrada is the leader of a large and violent Viking army. Along with Tostig — the brother of King Harold — this other Harold has invaded England. They aim to kill the king and seize power. You know that King Harold will beat them in a huge battle, but right now the Vikings are confident they'll thrash the English. Harold Hard-rada is more than happy to talk to you about the crook you're chasing.

"She was here," he tells you. "I saw her steal one of our longboats. Still, we won't need it. We're going to win this battle and settle down in England. Isn't that right, lads?" His men all shout, "Yes!" and bang their swords on their shields.

"Can you tell me where she may have gone?" you

ask him.

"Oh, she said something about a place called America, I think. Who cares? She's going to miss a really good fight, right, lads?"

"Right!" they all yell.

You decide it's time to beat a hasty retreat in case they want to use you for target practice. You hurry back to your Chronoskimmer at #34 to check out the clue you've just been given.

#127. As you head through the fields — the swampy land around the Isle of Ely — you're stopped by some English soldiers. They take you along to see their leader, Hereward the Wake, thinking you're a Norman spy. You explain to Hereward that you're looking for the crook who stole a Ming vase.

"We caught a thief," Hereward tells you. "We'd just sacked Peterborough, and we found this stranger trying to lift our loot. Take a look at him — it may be the man you're after."

His men lead you to a hut where they've kept the crook captive. Just as you arrive, he's digging his way out of the back of the hut. You and the guards grab him quickly. It's not the person you're looking for, but when you search him, you find a sheet of paper in his pocket. And on the paper is a list of the names and addresses of all of Carmen's gang!

If you think the Ming vase was stolen by:
Lotta Style —*go to #39*
Chips Motherboard —*go to #102*
Li Non Mee —*go to #73*
B. B. D. O'Brien —*go to #152*
Carl LaFong —*go to #22*
Alexander Graham Edison —*go to #115*
Benjamin Hama — *go to #140*
Sarah Nade —*go to #56*

#128. Socrates was the teacher of Plato and a great philosopher in his own right. He was most interested in ethics — the study of how people *should* behave. He so believed in obeying the law that when he was found guilty of a false charge against him, he stayed behind to face death rather than make an easy escape. Luckily, he's still alive when you find him. You ask him about the crook you're following.

"Thieves are not obedient to the law," he tells you. "I approve of your efforts to capture this crook. I can help by telling you that the brown-eyed woman mentioned that she was going forward in time from here. But not as far as the start of the Ming Dynasty."

You wish him luck with his own case and head back to the time machine at #19 to check up on these clues.

#129. The Chronoskimmer has landed you in China in the 14th century. But you're in the mountains of Tibet, known as the Roof of the World. There's nobody here because it's so cold. Better head to #72 before you freeze to death!

#130. The Chronoskimmer lands, and you climb out. You're in Mexico in the 16th century. The Aztecs are great builders of cities and temples, and they managed to do all of the work without ever using the wheel. Though they knew about it, they never bothered to make carts or anything with wheels to travel on or in. So they used sleds instead, or hundred of slaves.

The computer in your Chronoskimmer beeps to let you know it's finished scanning the area for clues. It has discovered that the thief who stole the Aztec temple was seen by three witnesses. The crook then fled to another time and country, but the computer is not sure which one, so it has given you three choices. If you question the witnesses, maybe they can tell you something that will help you track down the thief.

If you want to talk to:
Montezuma — go to #75
Cuitlahautzin — go to #54
Ahuizotl — go to #113

If you think the crook went to:
14th century China — go to #129
12th century Japan — go to #158
1st century B.C. Rome — go to #8

#131. You've tracked Sarah Nade to the palace of the caliph. She's managed to disguise herself as a dancing girl and has stolen the caliph's royal jewels! Thinking quickly, you grab a pipe from the hands of a snake charmer and start to play. Right in front of Sarah Nade, a snake pops out of its basket.

Sarah is terrified and faints, because she thinks the snake will bite her. What you know — and she doesn't — is that the snakes used in these acts have their poison removed to make them safe. While she's out cold, you recover the stolen jewels. You also find a map on her showing where she's hidden the stolen Viking longboat. Then you call up the Chief to tell him you've solved this case. "I'm a real charmer," you tell him.

"Congratulations," the Chief replies. "Well, you'd better add up your travel points and head for the back of the book to see if you've earned yourself that promotion!"

#132. You've landed in Greece in the 5th century B.C. There are a lot of great philosophers around — men who try to find out the meaning of life. Maybe they can help you find out why you're here. If not, you'd better go on to #72.

#133. You've trailed Chips Motherboard to an abacus factory. An abacus is a counting machine invented by the Chinese. It uses colored beads strung on wires and acts a little like a pocket calculator. But you've calculated wrongly, and Chips isn't here. You'd better move on to #111 to find out why you're in the wrong place.

#134. The Chronoskimmer sets you down in England in the 11th century. You've reached Sherwood Forest. One hundred years from now, Robin Hood will be making his men merry by robbing the Sheriff of Nottingham here. But unless you feel like hanging around a hundred years, you'd better get along to #72.

#135. The Chronoskimmer has landed you in Japan in the 12th century. It's a time of great progress for the country. The many islands that make up Japan have finally become united. The emperor and his court have become nothing more than showpieces, as the real power is now in the hands of a military ruler called the shogun. But literature, poetry, and painting are being created, some of which will become classics. And the Buddhist monks in the country are leading a religious revival.

The computer on your time machine beeps to tell you it's dug up some information.

If you want to question:
Shinran — go to #139
Eisai — go to #55
The Lady Murasaki — go to #1

If you think that the crook has fled to:
19th century West Africa — go to #29
16th century Mexico — go to #101
8th-12th-century Islamic world — go to #163.

#136. Cheng-Zi is the grandson of the Ming Emperor Hung Wu. He's going to become the second emperor, but he's not really a very good ruler. As a result, he'll be deposed. Right now, though, he's still just a prince — and not a very good prince, either. He doesn't seem to be able to do anything right. He does agree to see you, and you ask about the crook who stole the Ming vase.

"I saw him take it," he tells you. "I wondered if I should stop him, but I didn't know if he had Grandfather's permission to take the vase. I wouldn't want to arrest him if he had."

"But he didn't have permission," you reply.

"Well, I know it now," Cheng-Zi complains. "But not then. Anyway, the crook did say he was going back over a thousand years in the past from here."

With a sigh, you head back to your Chronoskimmer at #50 to check out this clue. No wonder Cheng-Zi will make a rotten emperor.

#137. You find that Omar Khayyám is really an astronomer and mathematician. He writes poetry just for fun. He's a very interesting and intense man, constantly working or scribbling notes. He forces himself to take a break when you ask him about the crook who stole the manuscript of his most famous poem, *The Rubáiyát*.

"I was working at the time," he explains. "And when I looked around, my manuscript was missing. I do recall somebody speaking to me who said that they were off to the Far East next."

You thank him for his help and promise to try your best to get his manuscript back for him. Then you head back to the time machine at #88 to check out the clue he gave you.

#138. The Chronoskimmer lands you in Mexico in the 16th century. But the Aztecs have swept through this area, and they've either captured or killed everyone. There's no one here to question, so you might as well head off to #72.

#139. Shinran was a pupil of the monk Honen, in 12th-century Japan. He helped to start the "Pure Land" Buddhist faith. Like Honen, he believed that Buddhism was for everyone, not just the monks. As a result, both men were persecuted by the powerful monks of their day. When you arrive, Shinran is quietly sitting and meditating. You wait till he's done, then ask him about the thief you're seeking.

"The woman you seek," he replies, "has gone from here. Her mind is not pure, and she still wants to steal. She has gone to a country to the west of Japan."

You thank him and let him continue his meditations in peace. You head back to your Chronoskimmer at #135 to check out this clue.

#140. You've followed Benjamin Hama to Brighton. In about 700 years the town will become very popular as a holiday spot. Unless you want to wait around for that to happen, you'd better move on to #111.

#141. The Chronoskimmer stops, and you land in China in the 14th century. The Ming Dynasty has just begun, and the Chinese have driven out the old Mongol invaders who had ruled the country for several hundred years. The Ming emperors will reform the country, introducing a lot of people to administer the people. To become one of these administrators, you have to pass an examination in Chinese classic literature. This is probably the oldest form of school test in history. You're just glad you don't have to take it!

The onboard computer beeps to let you know it's finished scanning for leads.

If you want to question:
Tien Shun — go to #103
Wang Chen — go to #57
Yesen — go to #124

If you think the crook went to:
11th century England — go to #161
5th century Greece B.C. — go to #19
16th century Mexico — go to #36

#142. You've traced Sarah Nade to the statue of Romulus and Remus with the wolf. According to the city's legend, the twin brothers were raised by a she-wolf. You don't think there's much truth to it, and there's not much to your search here, either. You'd better move on to #111.

#143. You find that Yahya ibn Khālid is the grand vizier. This is the right-hand man to the caliph, and the person in charge of the day-to-day running of everything. Yahya was also the teacher of Caliph Harūn ar-Rashid, and is a favorite of the ruler's. But he's very busy making sure that the palace is running smoothly. So busy, in fact, that he doesn't have time to talk to you. So you head back to your Chronoskimmer at #17 to follow up on another lead — with better luck next time, you hope!

#144. Crassus was a very rich politician in Rome in the 1st century B.C. He was also a partner of Julius Caesar and Pompey in ruling Rome. Later in his life he'll be sent to govern Syria. He'll lose a vital battle and be captured and killed by his enemies. When you arrive, though, he's still in Rome, counting some of his vast stores of money. You ask him about the thief you're trailing.

"Ssh!" he tells you nervously. "Don't talk about people like that! With all my money, I'm terribly afraid of those sort of people." You notice he won't even say the word *thief*! "Anyway, if it will help get rid of you, I did see that person. He spoke about going forward in time over a thousand years. Now, why don't you follow him and leave me in peace with my money?"

"You missed counting that one," you tell him. In a

panic, he starts all over again. You shake your head and leave for your Chronoskimmer at #77 to check on the clue you've been given.

#145. The Chronoskimmer lands you in West Africa in the 19th century. Many of the local people in this area belong to the Muslim faith. There's a religious revival going on, and the Muslims are coming to power all over the area. Many of the tribes are joining together in empires bigger than any that Africa has ever seen before.

The Chronoskimmer's computer has finished scanning the area and beeps.

If you want to question:
Adama — go to #48
Jajii Umar Tall — go to #116
Lowal — go to #169

If you think the thief escaped to:
14th century China — go to #27
12th century Japan — go to #65
16th century Mexico — go to #82

#146. You've landed in Rome in the 1st century B.C. The old style of government is fading away. The rule of the people through voting is changing into the rule of one man as emperor. The first man to become almost that powerful was Julius Caesar. His adopted son, Octavian, will become the first real Emperor of Rome, taking on the name of Augustus. Some people like the idea of an emperor, but many want to see the old republic restored.

Meanwhile, the computer has found some clues for you to investigate. It looks as if the crook is still here somewhere, but only one of three people knows for sure.

If you want to talk to:

Marc Antony — go to #117
Cicero — go to #49
Octavian — go to #154

#147. You've arrived in England in the 11th century. It's wet and it's cold, which is just about right — you're all wet, and the trail's gone cold. Go on to #72 to find out why you are in the wrong place.

#148. Shirquh is the uncle of Saladin, in the 12th-century Islamic world. He is a very famous warrior in his own right. He and his nephew often fight alongside each other. Shirquh is a big man, and he's polishing his sword when you find him. You ask about the crook you're hunting down.

"If I had seen the thief you mention," Shirquh tells you, "I would have used this sword to chop off his hands." He swings it down, and you shudder at the thought. "So that person is lucky I never did spot him."

You thank the warrior politely, then return to your time machine at #6. Maybe you'll have better luck with another lead — or at least someone without such a sharp sword!

#149. Lung Ch'ing is the 12th Ming emperor. During his eight-year reign the empire was probably at its peak. He ended the long war with Anda and introduced a lot of reforms. In fact, he's introducing some new ones right now and sends word that he's sorry, but he simply doesn't have time to see you. You head back to the Chronoskimmer at #27 and hope one of your other leads is more successful.

#150. Kokofu is one of the tribal leaders and supporter of the great Osei Tutu in 19th-century West Africa. He's a powerful man himself but admires his ruler and happily follows his orders. You ask him about the crook you're looking for.

"I saw the man," he tells you. "He spoke about going back in time. He said his trip would be of less than a thousand years."

You thank him for his help and hurry back to your time machine at #62 to check up on this clue.

#151. Tostig was not a very nice man. He had been made Earl of Northumbria by King Edward, but was so unpopular that the people of Northumbria forced the king to remove him. Then Tostig became even more annoying so he was banished. When Edward died and Harold was made king, Tostig was so furious that he joined forces with the Viking leader Harold Hardrada and attacked his own brother. In the end Tostig and the Vikings lost the battle. When you find him, he's still heading for the fight. You ask about the crook who stole the Viking longboat.

"Why should I care?" he asks. "It's nothing to me what she stole. Now, I'm very busy, so either buzz off or I'll have you executed."

"I wouldn't hang around such a rude man anyway," you tell him. Then you head back to the Chronoskimmer at #34, hoping one of the other people will be a bit more useful than Tostig has been.

#152. You've trailed B. B. D. O'Brien to Old Sarum. This is a hilltop town that's going to be abandoned soon. A cathedral will be built beside the river below the town and the townspeople will move down there to build a new town called Salisbury. You had better move, too, but to #111.

#153. Ibn Sina was one of the greatest medical writers of the Middle Ages, known to the Europeans as Avicenna. His book *The Canon of Medicine* was used by doctors all over the world for hundreds of years. He's a very wise man, and a busy one, but he takes a break to see you. You ask him about the crook who stole *The Rubáiyát*.

"I did see her," he tells you. "She managed to get away from me by climbing a wall. She said she was off to see a Great Wall next."

You thank him for his help and return to your time machine at #88 to check out this lead.

#154. During the 1st century B.C. in Rome, Octavian is the great-nephew of Julius Caesar and also his adopted son. After he and his friends avenged the murder of Caesar, Octavian managed to become sole ruler of the Roman Empire. He was the first and probably one of the best of the emperors. He made strong reforms, supported the arts and literature, and rebuilt the city of Rome as a splendid capital.

When you find him, he's still only the general who

will one day defeat Marc Antony in the great sea battle of Actium. He's in his bath, playing with his toy boats and planning his campaign. You're not allowed in to see him, so you head back to your Chronoskimmer at #146 to follow one of the other leads.

#155. Sophocles is a writer of tragic plays. His heroes and heroines always seem to die by the end of his plays. But the plays are well written and filled with poetry, so he is always popular. He is proud of this fact and keeps trying to show you all the awards he's won for his plays.

"Just the facts, please," you insist. "Did you see the thief I'm trailing?"

"Can't I show you just one first-place ribbon?" You shake your head no and Sophocles sighs. "Oh, all right. I saw the woman. She wouldn't look at my awards, either. Said she was hungry and wanted to eat some foreign food or other. Then she said she was going on a trip 1500 years into the future. And I thought I had a great imagination. Maybe she's going to be killed. Most of my heroines get killed. Did you know that? It stops the actresses asking me to write sequels."

You thank him and hurry back to your Chronoskimmer at #84 as fast as you can before he can start in about his awards again.

#156.   You've arrived in Japan in the 12th century. As you land, one of the frequent earthquakes starts shaking the country. You'd better get out of here fast and head for #72.

#157.   You've traced Sarah Nade to a rice paddy. It's filled with water and is terribly soggy. It's not the only thing that's damp — your spirits are, too. There's no sign of Sarah. Head for #111 to find out why you're in the wrong place.

#158.   The Chronoskimmer sets you down in Japan in the 12th century. Several hundred years of war have just been ended by one of the rival warlords declaring himself the shogun, or military ruler of the country. As a result, a sort of uneasy peace has settled over Japan. The shogun aims to solve a lot of the troubles that have been caused by the wars — famine, plagues, and wandering bands of soldier-monks that loot and pillage.

The Chronoskimmer's computer beeps, letting you know it's found some leads.

If you want to question:

Honen—go to #83

Hojo Tokimasa — go to #41

Dogen — go to #162   ☞

If you think that the crook went on to:
8th-12th-century Islamic world — go to #24
11th -century England — go to #134
19th century West Africa — go to #62

#159. Martín Cortés is the son of the famous explorer. He's a young man, but determined to follow in his father's footsteps and explore new lands. You ask him about the crook you're chasing. He shrugs.

"All I know is she was going somewhere in Asia. That's no fun. She should stay here and explore, like my dad. He's the best in the world."

"That's the spirit," you agree. Then you head back to your time machine at #105 to check out this clue.

#160. It's 11th-century England. Odo is the half brother of William the Conqueror. William had him made a bishop, and he enjoys the job. To celebrate his brother's victory at Hastings, Odo had a great tapestry made. Called the Bayeux Tapestry (after the cathedral where it was placed), it is 231 feet long. You ask him about the villain you're after.

"Sorry, no time," he replies. "I've got to get this tapestry finished. Do you have any idea what hard work this is?"

You're not going to get any help from him, that's for sure. He may even ask you to pitch in and help! Time to return to the Chronoskimmer at #110 and try a different lead!

#161. You've reached England in the 11th century. As you look around, an arrow whistles past your ear and thuds into a tree. You see there's a note attached to it, which you read. It says: *Go straight to #72.* And it's signed by the Chief!

#162. Dogen is a monk in the 13th century who brought Zen Buddhism to Japan. He stressed the need to meditate by sitting cross-legged on the floor and emptying the mind. When you arrive, he's just finished a class with his students, so he's free to talk to you.

"The person you seek," he tells you, "was here. He is going on to meet a group of Muslims who practice a religion called Islam. Most interesting."

You thank him for his help. "Hope your knees don't hurt from all that sitting cross-legged," you tell him. Then you return to your time machine at #158 to check out this clue.

#163. The Chronoskimmer has landed you in the Islamic world in the 8th–12th centuries. It's a time of great expansion for the empire, but the only thing expanding for you is your embarrassment. You're in the wrong place. Better go straight to #72.

#164. You land in England in the 11th century. As you arrive, so does William the Conqueror's fleet. If you don't want to get arrested as a spy, you'd better rush to #72.

#165. You've reached Mexico in the 16th century. You've landed on a temple of sacrifice. You'll be the next victim if you don't make a quick escape to #72.

#166. You've tracked Benjamin Hama to the food market in Rome. There are plenty of things to eat — quails and snails, sheep's eyes and peacocks . . . But no sign of Bennie. You'd better go on to #111 now.

#167. You've chased Li Non Mee to a harem. This is the part of the royal palace where all of the ruler's wives live. No outsiders can get in. If you don't want to be executed by the guards, you'd better flee to #111.

#168. The Chronoskimmer comes to a halt, and you've reached Rome in the 1st century B.C. It's the height of Roman civilization. Many writers and poets live at this time. The Emperor Augustus loves to spend money to encourage the arts. Another popular form of expression is public speaking, and there are many men known from this time who were considered to be great speakers. You can only hope one of them can tell you what you'd love to hear about the crook you're seeking!

The Chronoskimmer's computer beeps to tell you it's finished checking for leads. It has three people you could question and three possible places the crook may have gone.

If you want to speak to:
Livy — *go to #43*
Horace — *go to #10*
Virgil — *go to #85*

If you think the villain went to:
11th century England — *go to #164*
16th century Mexico — *go to #52*
5th century B.C. Greece — *go to #123*

#169. You've landed in 19th-century West Africa. Lowal is one of the four sons of the chief Adama. All four sons will rule Adamwa after Adama dies. Lowal is getting educated on how to become a king. He's glad to take a break from his lessons when you ask him about the crook you're chasing.

"She said she was going somewhere that's five hundred years in the past," he tells you.

You thank him for his help and head back to your time machine at #145 to follow up on this clue.

#170.   The Chronoskimmer lands you in Mexico in the 16th century. Mexico City is being burned down by the Spanish invaders. If you want to escape the flames, you'd better take a quick trip to #72.

SCORING CHART

Add up all of your travel points (you did remember to mark one point for each time you moved to a new number, didn't you?). If you have penalty points for trying to arrest the wrong person, add those in, too. Then check your score against the chart below to see how you did.

0 – 17: You couldn't really have solved these cases in these few steps. Either you're boasting about your abilities or you're actually working with Carmen's gang. Be honest and try again —if you dare!

18 – 40: Super sleuth! You work very well and don't waste time. Well done — you deserve the new rank and the nice big bonus you'll get next payday!

41 – 60: Private eye material! You're a good, steady worker, and you get your man (or woman). Still, there's room for improvement, and you can always try again to get another promotion.

☞

61 – 80: Detective first class. You're not a world-famous private eye yet, but you're getting there. Try again and see if you can move up a grade or two!

81 – 100: Rookie material. You're taking too long to track down the crooks. Next time they're going to get away from you. Try a little harder and see if you're really better than this.

Over 100: Are you sure you're really cut out to be a detective? Maybe you'd be better off looking for an easier job — a janitor for Acme, maybe? Still, if you're determined to be a detective, why not try again and see if this was just an off day. Better luck next time!